Advance Praise for

My Red Hat Grandma and Me

"This book is a must for all children, especially in today's society. It addresses all the critical elements for healthy social and emotional development, which is the primary predictor of success in life. The cornerstone of a secure attachment, namely, unconditional love, comes alive in the world of Red Hat Grandma and Kit."

> **Ella H. Pecsok, Ph.D.**
> **Clinical Neuropsychologist, Norfolk, VA**

"An age appropriate and lovely story, *My Red Hat Grandma and Me* creates a lot of teachable moments! I look forward to the next book to see what Kit will learn!"

> **Sarah Singer, Director,**
> **Emmanuel Episcopal Day School, Virginia Beach, VA**

"I love this book. *My Red Hat Grandma and Me* makes children feel good, wanted, and loved. This charming book mirrors the same kind of bond that exists between my "perfect" grandchildren and me."

> **Lucille Stubbs, ATR-BC, LPC, LMFT**
> **Marriage and Family Counselor**
> **Owner, Awakening Therapies, Virginia Beach, VA**

"Oh, what a delightful child! Oh, what a precious Grandma! Hilda Principe's *My Red Hat Grandma and Me* will provide so many sweet memories for so many grandparents, parents, and children. A must-have book for the little ones we love."

> **Marti Drummond-Dale, Adjunct, Old Dominion University,**
> **Darden College Of Education, Norfolk, VA**
> **And "Nana" to Sadie Ann, Daniel Patrick, and Liam Ryland!**

Hilda Principe

my Red Hat Grandma & me

Tate Publishing & Enterprises

The inspiration for Kit's Red Hat Grandma is my own wonderful grandmother, Beatrice Johnson Myers. She made the kitchen warm, the quilts cozy, and a little granddaughter secure and happy. I hope you are looking down from Heaven, Grandmother, because this one's for you.

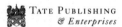
TATE PUBLISHING
& Enterprises

Tate Publishing is committed to excellence in the publishing industry. Our staff of highly trained professionals, including editors, graphic designers, and marketing personnel, work together to produce the very finest books available. The company reflects the philosophy established by the founders, based on Psalms 68:11,

"THE LORD GAVE THE WORD AND GREAT WAS THE COMPANY OF THOSE WHO PUBLISHED IT."

If you would like further information, please contact us:
1.888.361.9473 | www.tatepublishing.com
TATE PUBLISHING & Enterprises, LLC | 127 E. Trade Center Terrace
Mustang, Oklahoma 73064 USA

Published in the United States of America
ISBN: 978-1-5988699-0-3
07.03.13

Acknowledgements

My Grandma Atry loved red and purple. Her loving, grand-child-doting personality is the heart of *My Red Hat Grandma*. I think there is a little of her in all grandmas.

Many wonderful people have blessed my life with their presence. My precious husband, Martin, believed in me and always encouraged me, whatever my endeavors. My children, Dawn Stephenson and Steven Wells, were, and still are, what all children should be: loving, kind and wonderful. My sister, Linda Starkey, is my only sibling and is the best sister a gal can have. I am thankful we share DNA. My grandson, Connor Stephenson, is my inspiration for all of Red Hat Grandma's grandchildren.

My blessings are too numerous to count, and I am extremely fortunate to be able to say that. Some of my blessings have names and these are just a few of them: Martha Drummond-Dale, Bess Mann, Grace Grant, Didema Dagenhart, Ann Crosswhite, Mary Rybaczuk, Esther Clark, and Carol Ann Oporto. They are all friends of many years, and they exemplify the spirits of "red and purple" women all over the world. Most of these women taught school with me; all are nurturers of children.

I want to add a huge "thank you" to Tate Publishing. They have been wonderful to work with and shared my enthusiasm for Red Hat Grandma and her love of children. A special thanks to the staff with whom I have worked. They always returned my calls and never failed in their roles as "cheerleaders" and "enthusiastic supporters" as they guided me through the unfamiliar maze of the publishing world.

Now, I try to live up to my Red Hat Grandma's example of what a grandma should be. I hope you enjoy her and her family as the grandchildren grow through the years.

My name is Kit,
and I just now turned four.
My face is all covered in
freckles galore.
I have bright **red** pigtails
my mom ties with **red** bows,
and I often wear dresses
that my grandma sews.

I stay with my grandma

during the day, so I don't mind

my parents going away.

My mommy & daddy

go to work in the town,

while I **hopscotch** and **jump rope**

and play "all fall down!"

My grandma wears

Purple
& Red

every day.

I wonder if **all grandmas**

dress up that way?

Grandma has so many
hats, scarves, purses, and shoes,
it's a good thing she has me
to help her to choose.

On Grandma's bed sits
Sara, the stuffed bear.
Her sweater is purple;
red bows in her hair.

I play with Sara
and have tea parties sometimes,
and I wear the red beads
Grandma says are all mine.

I love my grandma because she's so nice.
We dance and laugh as we sing "Three Blind Mice."

She **plays** with me, **rocks** me,
and **sings** to me too.
And when it's naptime,
she knows just what to do.

We kneel together
and she teaches me to pray
just like she taught Daddy
to pray the same way.

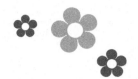

She says God will love me
no matter what,
and I know that it's true 'cause

He loves
me a lot!

Sometimes I act **naughty**;

sometimes my eyes cry.

Sometimes I throw tantrums

or tell a **little lie**.

But Grandma gives hugs
that say she forgives.

Grandma's hugs are always
where *forgiveness* lives.

I love my sweet grandma
because she tells me
how **precious** I am,
and I'm sweet
as can be.

She makes me feel **good**
and that makes me feel **glad**.
I thank God in my prayers
for Grandma,
Mom, & Dad.

e|LIVE

---

listen|imagine|view|experience

AUDIO BOOK DOWNLOAD INCLUDED WITH THIS BOOK!

In your hands you hold a complete digital entertainment package. Besides purchasing the paper version of this book, this book includes a free download of the audio version of this book. Simply use the code listed below when visiting our website. Once downloaded to your computer, you can listen to the book through your computer's speakers, burn it to an audio CD or save the file to your portable music device (such as Apple's popular iPod) and listen on the go!

How to get your free audio book digital download:

1. Visit www.tatepublishing.com and click on the e|LIVE logo on the home page.
2. Enter the following coupon code:
   84f4-0392-ec8c-a824-2926-3d30-bfc3-edd8
3. Download the audio book from your e|LIVE digital locker and begin enjoying your new digital entertainment package today!